Mr. Astley's Blueberries

Kelly Jenkins Lin

ILLUSTRATED BY
Samantha Lane Fiddy

Published by Three Flower Farm Press

Mr. Astley's Blueberries
Text copyright © 2012 by Kelly Jenkins Lin
Illustrations copyright © 2012 by Samantha Lane Fiddy
All rights reserved.

First Edition—2012 / Designed by Jaywalker Studios LLC

This is Mr. Astley and these are his blueberries.

Mr. Astley lives at the end of a long, winding lane, in a small white house with green shutters and a blue shed out back. It is a quiet place, nestled deep in the woods. There is plenty of sunlight and a small stream nearby. "Just right for blueberries," Mr. Astley says with a smile.

Every February, when most people only dream of blueberries, Mr. Astley puts on his boots, his hat, his mittens, and his scarf and heads out to the blueberry patch.

After studying each bush, he snips and he cuts, trimming a little bit here and a little bit there until, at last, with a big pile of branches beside him, Mr. Astley stands back and says, "That ought to do it," and goes inside to get warm.

Next, Mr. Astley inspects the fence around the
blueberries, checking to make sure an animal hasn't
made a hole in it or dug underneath it. Once, when
Mr. Astley was working on his fence, he heard a
thrashing noise coming from the woods.

Standing up to see what all the fuss was about, Mr. Astley was just in time to see a deer leap over one side of the fence before crashing through on the other. "That won't do," he said and set about building a taller fence.

In April, when the white, star-shaped blossoms begin to bloom, birds flock to Mr. Astley's yard. One day, Mr. Astley counted as many as fifty birds! To keep the birds from eating all the berries, Mr. Astley stretches a great big net over the patch. It is a dickens of a job! The net tangles easily and catches on buttons and hats if he isn't careful.

Still, every now and then a bird
gets in and eats some berries.

"That's all right," Mr. Astley
says with a wink, "there's
enough to go around."

Throughout the spring and summer, as the berries turn from green to red to blue, all sorts of animals make their way to Mr. Astley's yard, coyotes and chipmunks, groundhogs and squirrels, even skunks. Sometimes, a dragonfly will get its colorful wings caught in the net, trapping the dragonfly inside. When that happens, Mr. Astley very carefully pulls the net back and frees the dragonfly's wings. "You're welcome," Mr. Astley says as the happy dragonfly flies away.

In June, when the berries are almost ready to be picked, Mr. Astley takes two lawn chairs from his shed, one red and one blue, and sets them up beside the blueberry patch. When evening comes, he and his daughter take their tea outside and sit. Before long, something wonderful — something truly amazing — happens!

Hundreds of them appear like stars twinkling over the blueberries.
"I think I'll call this place 'Lightning Bug Blues,'" Mr. Astley said to
his daughter the first time he saw them.

At last, it is time to pick the berries. Mr. Astley and his daughter put on their shorts and their sneakers, their sunhats, and bug spray, and head out to the blueberry patch. Mr. Astley picks berries from the low branches while his daughter, who sometimes has to stand on a crate, reaches for the berries at the top. "Those are the best," she says, her mouth full of berries.

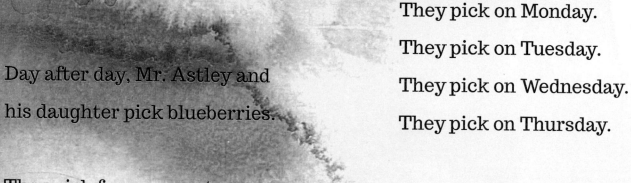

Day after day, Mr. Astley and his daughter pick blueberries.

They pick from sunup to sundown, up one row and down the next.

They pick on Sunday.

They pick on Monday.

They pick on Tuesday.

They pick on Wednesday.

They pick on Thursday.

It is hard work, but still they pick.

"There's no time for rest during blueberry season," Mr. Astley says with a grimace.

On Friday, Mr. Astley goes inside to sort the berries. Ripe, juicy blue ones go into wooden baskets. Small red ones go to the compost pile to make more blueberries next year. Then, on Saturday, Mr. Astley and his daughter put the baskets of berries into the back of their car and head to the farmers' market. "These are the best blueberries yet," they say, and nod in agreement.

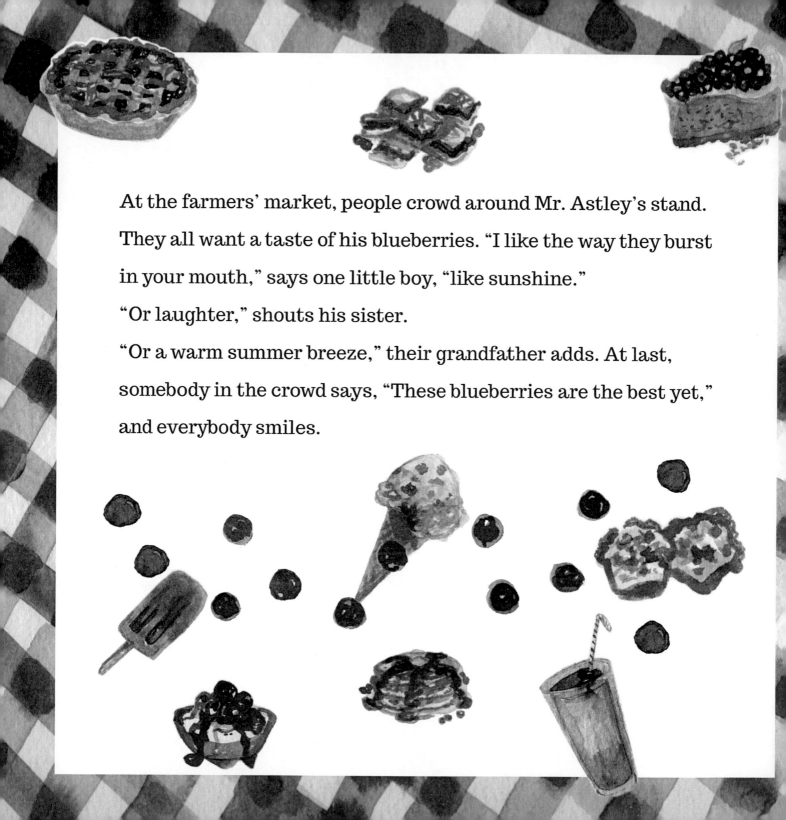

At the farmers' market, people crowd around Mr. Astley's stand. They all want a taste of his blueberries. "I like the way they burst in your mouth," says one little boy, "like sunshine."

"Or laughter," shouts his sister.

"Or a warm summer breeze," their grandfather adds. At last, somebody in the crowd says, "These blueberries are the best yet," and everybody smiles.

In September, Mr. Astley folds up his chairs and stacks the empty baskets. Next he hangs up his pruning shears and puts away his gloves. Finally, Mr. Astley takes down the net, being careful not to catch it on anything, and checks the fence one last time. As he works, birds hover overhead and animals watch from the woods. "See you next year," Mr. Astley says and goes inside.

When the snow begins to fall, Mr. Astley puts on his boots, his hat, and his mittens and takes his camera out to the blueberry patch. The berries are all gone and the leaves have long since dropped to the ground or been carried away by the wind. Still there is something beautiful about the bushes, their bright red branches covered with a dusting of snow. "Wow!" Mr. Astley says before taking a picture.

In January, Mr. Astley walks to his mailbox. Reaching past the bills and the magazines he finds what he's looking for, a brand new nursery catalog. It is full of all kinds of blueberry bushes along with all sorts of suggestions about where to plant them and how to take care of them. Sitting by the fire, Mr. Astley pores over the pages again and again. "So many choices," he says, scratching his head.

When at last spring comes and the ground thaws, Mr. Astley takes his new bushes and carefully places them in the ground. Stepping back, he leans on his shovel, wipes his brow and says, "These will be the best blueberries yet."

And they will be.

All royalties from the sale of this book will be donated to the Lauren Dunne Astley Memorial Fund, dedicated to promoting dynamic educational programs, particularly those in the areas of the development of healthy teen relationships, the arts, and community service.

For more information, visit laurendunneastleymemorialfund.org.

51653827R00021